Annie Wood Besant

Charles Bradlaugh

A sketch of his life and work

Annie Wood Besant

Charles Bradlaugh
A sketch of his life and work

ISBN/EAN: 9783337097653

Printed in Europe, USA, Canada, Australia, Japan

Cover: Foto ©Raphael Reischuk / pixelio.de

More available books at **www.hansebooks.com**

CHARLES BRADLAUGH

A SKETCH OF

His Life and Work.

BY

ANNIE BESANT.

SAN FRANCISCO:

THE READER'S LIBRARY.

1203 Market Street.

Issued Monthly.   Subscription, $3.00 per year.

VOL. 1.   JULY, 1891.   NO. 1.

CHARLES BRADLAUGH.

By MRS. ANNIE BESANT.

INTRODUCTORY.

The character sketch for this month has been fortunately intrusted to the hands of the person who of all others was most competent to perform the task. Mrs. Annie Besant, his comrade for years, knew Mr. Bradlaugh better than almost any other living man or woman. Mr. Bradlaugh's estimate of her ability and her sympathy was expressed by him shortly before he died in an article written for the American press, from which the following are extracts :

"Mrs. Annie Besant as an orator has few, if any, equals amongst her own sex on either side of the Atlantic. In 1877, on the occasion of her trial, jointly with myself, for publishing the Knowlton *pamphlet, Lord Chief Justice Cockburn paid such tribute to Mrs. Besant for her talent as an advocate as is probably without parallel from judge to prisoner in the records of English trials.

"To compensate her for the enforced loneliness of her home, Mrs. Besant's ever-restless mind, from 1877 until 1890, has so constantly sought additional toil, that it is wonderful she has survived the incessant struggle.

"For ten years, as my partner in publishing and co-editor with me, our work was common, our standpoint on all speculative matters was the same. She was devotion itself,

---

* " Fruits of Philosophy."

enduring much, and always ready to labor and to suffer, and I have sometimes sorely regretted that my Parliamentary work broke our paths somewhat in twain. During the past four or five years her sympathies have led her to take views of the remedies for social misery in which I cannot concur ; and she has found guidance to a mysticism which seems to me unsound and unreal. But of this I am sure, that, with Lessing, she always seeks for truth, and will never hesitate, whatever the personal consequence, to proclaim in turn each truth she thinks she has found."

This Character Sketch, written by her when the grave had but closed over Mr. Bradlaugh, does not profess to be an impartial summing up of his life's work. Partisan journalists of the baser sort have done their worst for years to defile this man's name, and to represent him as a kind of unclean Yahoo, full of blasphemy and sedition. Mrs. Besant's picture, painted from life, comes as a useful corrective to the malignant attacks of bigoted opponents. No doubt Mr. Bradlaugh said very much that was painful, even revolting, to the reverent mind. But what Christian is there who, on reading over the shameful story of intolerance with which Mr. Bradlaugh was treated, does not feel that the responsibility for much that was most deplorable in Mr. Bradlaugh's teaching, lies at the door, not of the Freethinker, but of the un-Christlike Christian of our time. That this resolute soul lived and died doing so much good work for the poor and the oppressed, although without the conscious inspiration of Christianity, should surely not be reckoned so much a reproach to him as to those blind leaders of the blind, whose bigotry and stupidity drove him outside the fold.

—Editor.

MOST certainly I do not pretend that this sketch of my dear friend will be an "impartial" one. True, we may see faults in a friend, and because we see them claim that we are impartial judges of his character, but that is a mere self-delusion. Everybody knows how different are our friend's faults from the faults of our enemy ; in the one they are the mere shadings that serve to show up the lights of the character, in the other they are dark stains marring all beauty. Where there is strong personal affection, impartiality is a mere *façon de parler ;* we do not judge our friends, we love them.

Especially difficult is it for any of his contemporaries to judge rightly of Charles Bradlaugh. His vivid and intense personality, his imperious will, his imposing physique, acted strongly on every one who came in contact with him ; all he touched became either his friends or his foes. None who knew him remained indifferent to him ; he aroused bitterer hatred against himself than did any other man of his time, and he awoke more passionate enthusiasm and devoted love. There are men of his own age, and men older than he is—he who will never grow any older now—rough men, battered by toil and hardened by lives of conflict and sour endurance, who were rendered prostrate by the intelligence of his death, and cannot rally even to the work on which their bread depends. Not to many is it given thus to bind men's hearts to his own so closely, that when his breaks in death theirs break in sorrow. Yet thus it was with this dead man. Impartial judgment cannot yet go forth and stamp its verdict on his life. But far on in the twentieth century, when all our feuds are hushed and our quarrels still, when burning questions are cold and noisy controversies lie silent as that Woking grave, then shall History with her calm

eyes, free of passion, read the record of this ended life,
speak her judgment on the work he wrought for his nation ;
and methinks that then his memory shall pass to her right
hand, not her left, and shine forever as a star in the con-
stellations of England's deathless dead.

———

Back in the thirties—more exactly on September 26,
1833—in Bacchus Walk, Hoxton, the baby who was to be
Charles Bradlaugh saw the light of the world that was to
offer him so hard a problem. Father, a solicitor's clerk,
poor and mediocre ; mother a gentle, commonplace woman,
so far as I have been able to gather. Neither the one nor
the other seems to have made a very strong impression on
the lad, who was as a young eagle in a barn fowl's nest. The
father was fond of fishing, touching at this one point his remarkable son. Good people of an ordinary type—such is
the general faint impression left on my mind about them.
His sisters are gentle, sweet-natured women, who have
never had any real chance in life, and who will sorely miss
the always gentle, helpful brother, who had gone so far
away from them and theirs, but never forgot the tie of kin-
dred and affection. In his strong intellect, marked personality, and persistent energy, in all the proportions of his
virile strength, he stands as much apart from his own family as from average men and women, offering as perplexing
a problem to those who see in the individual nothing more
than the outcome of physical heredity as they could well
essay to solve.

When little Charles Bradlaugh was old enough to learn
his A B C, he was sent to Abbey Street National School,
Bethnal Green, and from that he went to a boys' school in
Coldharbor street, Hackney Road. At the age of eleven
his exiguous education was finished, so far as his parents were

concerned, for the lad was needed to help to keep the home together ; but he had already begun to educate himself, and was his own best teacher for the rest of his life. This self-education began with a copy of Cobbett's "Political Grid-iron," found among his father's books, and Charles Brad-laugh, *ætat* ten, laid this as the first brick of his edifice of self-culture. A half-penny was soon after expended on "The Charter," and behold him launched on the waves of radicalism, which he navigated during the whole remainder of his life. |

From twelve to fourteen, Charles Bradlaugh was an er-rand boy in the office in which his father was employed, and at fourteen he became wharf clerk and cashier at a coal merchant's. While thus employed his education progressed rapidly ; the great surge of the Chartist movement caught him up and touched the boy's ardent nature to enthusiasm ; never did he lose the love then acquired for the ringing songs of Ernest Jones and the rhymes of Ebenezer Elliott. He began in real earnest to study, to think. He was too poor to buy books, and his scanty wages were needed at home, but he would stand at the bookstall of some good-natured second-hand bookseller and devour some pages of a political treatise, returning day after day to resume the reading till the contents of the book were safely lodged in his most adhesive memory. Figure the boy's disappoint-ment when some thoughtless person, with pockets better lined than his, came along and bought the book, and so put sudden ending to the study. But now and then a book was bought, hardly and slowly earned, a few pence at a time, when the boy was sent an errand and omnibus fare given, and he raced away, his long legs skimming over the ground faster than any omnibus could carry him, that he might not wrong his employer of his time, but might save the pennies to buy some coveted book. "Vocabularies and dictionaries I used to buy," he has said to me, "for I could get most out of them." And then he would buy a stray candle and sit up conning his treasured books.

HOW HE BECAME A FREETHINKER.

But now another great step was to be taken. His political education was bowling along merrily under the impetus of Chartist meetings ; his theological education was to receive a stimulus in its turn. Charles Bradlaugh was earnest in his religion as in everything else ; in him all the motive springs of life quivered with passion, and however sternly dominant the intellect, every conviction burned like a fire within him. He could never hold a belief half-heartedly, and the germs of that intensity of the man were in the boy. Chosen to prepare for confirmation, as one of the most promising of his young flock, by the Rev. John Graham Packer, clergyman of his parish church, St. Peter's, Hackney Road, he must needs study the Thirty-nine Articles and compare them with the New Testament. Alas for the boy ! he found contradictions that puzzled him, and in no spirit of skepticism, but simply desiring help and explanation, he wrote to Mr. Packer and explained his difficulties. That this boy of fourteen, who was expected to do credit to his spiritual pastor, should try to understand instead of learning, was too much for the reverend gentleman's patience. He wrote to the parents, denouncing the lad as an atheist, and suspended him for three months from his office as teacher in the Sunday school. This treatment offered no solution to the perplexities in which young Bradlaugh was involved, but it did drive him in the direction of freethought, for, too proud to attend the church while excluded from the school, he betook himself to Bonner's Fields, where political and religious discussions were held on Sundays. He soon began to take part in these, defending Christianity against its assailants, but losing, bit by bit, in argument, the faith which Mr. Packer maintained only by terrorism. So things went on, and the end of the three months did not see the teacher back in the Sunday school ; and months passed over, and the old beliefs crumbled away. A debate on the "Inspiration of the Bible," in 1849, gave the *coup de grace* to his boyish faith ; he suffered and struggled and prayed, but all in vain ; he clung to his religion, but it melted away beneath his grasp. At last, towards the end of 1849, he made one last attempt. He had been studying Robert Taylor's "Diegesis," and he asked Mr. Packer to help him to find some answer to it. But Mr. Packer still "owned no argument but force," and the fact that this pertinaciously inquiring lad of sixteen had filled up the measure of his sins by becoming a teetotaler, rendered desperate the irate cleric. He persuaded his employers to give him three days in which "to change his opinions or lose his situation "—taking the very means to stereotype the boy in his views. Even then, Charles Bradlaugh did not know how to hesitate between personal advantage and honesty of life. He stood to his opinions and lost his situation, and went out alone into the world, outcast from home, knowing not how to earn his bread, a boy in his seventeenth year ; but in his dauntlessness, his honesty, his determination to be true at any cost, he was even then the Charles Bradlaugh whose watchword was "Thorough " all through his gallant life.

HIS YOUTHFUL STRUGGLES.

Now came an interlude in the way of an industrial career of a microscopic and short-lived kind. An old Chartist gave the young outcast shelter for a week, and during this week he started as a coal merchant. But as he had no money to buy coals, he had to sell them before he could buy them, an upside-down way of conducting a business which, while it avoided the danger of bad debts, did not lead to an extended trade. Still he had one good customer, a baker's wife, the commission on whose orders amounted to 10s. a week. Alack! The good soul learned that her youthful coal merchant was an infidel, and after subjecting him to a searching cross-examination, she declined further dealings. "I should be afraid my bread would smell of brimstone," she declared, and not a lump more of coal would she have. The coal business perished, consumed in the flame of the burning orthodoxy of the baker's wife, and after some further struggling, young Bradlaugh found a job of selling buckskin braces on commission. Meanwhile he was lodging with the widow of Richard Carlile, a good and staunch-hearted woman, of whom he always spoke with deep respect and gratitude. Here he learned French with Mrs. Carlile's children, varying the proceedings by falling desperately in love with Hypatia Carlile, and also diligently studied Hebrew, Greek and Arabic. On Sundays he trained his tongue in speech, and soon became known as "the boy orator," speaking much on religion and taking active part in the sympathetic movements in favor of Polish and Hungarian liberty. He grew tall, gaunt and thin, with long arms and legs protruding shamelessly from too brief garments. With humorous pathos in his later years he would describe the dismay with which he found his trousers ascending towards his knees, and his sleeves crawling towards his elbows, while his toes threatened emergence through his boots, declaring that he had never discovered the secret of the children of Israel, who had worn the same shoes for forty years without wearing them out.

Despite all his struggles, the lad got into debt, and his pain amounted to agony when some friendly Freethinkers, seeing his poverty, made among themselves a small subscription for him. This well-meant kindness touched him in his most sensitive spot, his pride and independence, and as he walked along near Charing Cross, seeing a poster offering a bounty of £6 10s. to recruits for the East India service, he walked to the place indicated and offered himself as a recruit. He was accepted, but presently, to his astonishment, found himself enrolled in the 50th Foot of her Majesty's army, instead of in the service of the Honorable East India Company. It appeared that one sergeant owed a man to the other, and paid over Bradlaugh to discharge his liability ; but Bradlaugh objected to being treated as a chattel, and proved so determined that he was allowed to choose, within the limits of the English army, what regiment he should be drafted into, and selected the 7th Dragoon Guards. So there he was, in 1850, at seventeen, a recruit in the red jacket, surely the very oddest member of her Majesty's forces.

Mr. Bradlaugh liked nothing better, when in a talkative mood, than to describe his experiences in the " Old Seventh : " his efforts at cooking, the wisdom of over-boiling rather than underboiling your potatoes, in case your evil cookery should lead to your being pelted with them ; his struggles with a troop-horse who knew more than a man, and who would jump forward or backward, present his head where his tail should be, and otherwise mock at the untrained lanky boy, who understood soldiering so much less than he did himself. Our recruit soon made his way into the trust and even the affection of his comrades, as he did all his life long with those among whom he worked ;

but his first days were not happy ones ; they were spent in
a sailing vessel, which took him and his fellow-recruits
from London to Dublin, and he was very sea-sick and ill at
ease with his comrades. They mocked him for his shabby
clothes of faded black ; they broke open his box, pulled out
his books, kicked his Greek lexicon to pieces, and nearly
doomed his Arabic vocabulary to the same fate.

THE SEA-SICK RECRUIT.

He was too heart-sick and too sea-sick to defend his
property, and would have left the ship with very little glory
had it not been for an incident that touched his sense of
justice. A storm arose, and, it being necessary to shift the
cargo, the captain offered the recruits £5 for their help.
The task over, and the storm passed, the captain refused to
give the money ; there were murmurs, but no one dared to
face the captain on his own ship, when suddenly the lanky
sea-sick lad sprang from the crowd, and poured out on the
astonished captain a flood of indignant eloquence, reproach-
ing him for his meanness and finally threatening him with
a letter to the *Times*. The captain capitulated before the
vehement orator, and paid the promised gratuity, the
equally amazed recruits discovering that the lad who had
seemed so helpless was by no means the fool he looked.
Still, the early days were not so smooth ; he annoyed the
officers by being a stickler for the Queen's Regulations, and
amused the men by his clumsiness at drill—the sense that
he was compelled to learn taking all the force and energy
out of him. A fight with a bully, who was also a good
boxer, was one of his early steps to popularity. He fought,
expecting to be beaten, but found that when he could hit
his enemy the enemy was obliged to fall down. Thence-
forth disregarding all blows aimed at himself, he knocked
his opponent down as often as he could, and finally, to his

great surprise, found out that he had won. "No one can stand against a blow of 'Leaves,'" was the verdict, "but you're a fool to get in the way of his fist."

SOME EXPLOITS OF "LEAVES."

"Leaves" was his regimental *soubriquet*, for he drank only tea and was always reading books, and when they found that being a teetotaler and a student did not prevent him from exhibiting exceptional physical courage, and from often standing between them and unfair treatment, the name of "Leaves" became one of affection instead of contempt.

On one or two occasions, however, he nearly came to grief. At Rathmines the clergyman of the parish preached a sermon, which was, he said, above the heads of the soldiers present. This annoyed Private Bradlaugh, and he wrote to the preacher, criticising the sermon and pointing to various blunders contained therein. On the following Sunday the regiment marched to church as usual, but "Leaves" and his comrades were prepared for action if any further insolence should be shown in the pulpit. A contemptuous sentence began, and in a moment three hundred heavy cavalry sabres smote the floor, unhooked and allowed to fall in one mighty crash. An inquiry was ordered, and Private Bradlaugh was summoned, but luckily, the Duke of Cambridge came to hold a review, and no further action was taken.

The other occasion was even more critical. He was orderly-room clerk, and a newly-arrived young officer came into the room where he was sitting at work, and addressed to him some discourteous order. Private Bradlaugh took no notice. The order was repeated with an oath. Still no movement. Then it came again, with some foul words added. The young soldier arose, drew himself to his full height, and walking up to the officer, bade him leave the room, or he would throw him out. The officer went, but in a few moments the grounding of muskets was heard outside, the door opened, and the Colonel walked in, accompanied by the officer. It was clear that the private soldier had committed an act for which he might be court-martialed, and as he said once, "I felt myself in a tight place." The officer made his accusation, and Private Bradlaugh was bidden to explain. He asked that the officer should state the exact words in which he had addressed him, and the officer who had, after all, a touch of honor in him, gave the offensive sentence, word for work. Then Private Bradlaugh said, addressing his Colonel, that the officer's memory must surely be at fault in the whole matter, as he could not have used language so unbecoming an officer and a gentleman. The Colonel turned to the officer with the dry remark : "I think Private Bradlaugh is right ; there *must* be some mistake," and he left the room.

HIS LIFE IN THE ARMY.

As orderly clerk, " Leaves " had a pleasant time enough. He used to read at night, putting his candle into the muzzle of his gun—a reprehensible practice, as he confessed in years when more convenient candlesticks were forthcoming. He became a capital rider, when he was not forced to learn, and got on excellent and affectionate terms with his old equine antagonist, teaching it various tricks which tended to the hilarity more than to the orderly drill of the regiment. He also grew into an admirable swordsman, gaining a dexterity that in later years often stood him in good stead, and up to 1885 the sword exercise was a favorite amusement with him. It was worth while to see him, as a magnificent specimen of physical vigor, with the heavy cavalry sabre in his hand, whirling it round his head, making tremendous cuts to right and left, lunging forward with astonishing reach, with lips close pressed, eyes flashing, face and form alive, instinct with energy and fire ; ah me ! all passed away now, helpless in narrow coffin with the earth heaped over him !

Ere his soldier-life came to an end in the summer of 1853—when he bought himself out· with a small legacy that came to him—a curiously characteristic act made him the hero of the Inniscarra peasantry. A land-owner had put up a gate across a right of way, closing it against soldiers and peasants, while letting the gentry pass through it. " Leaves " looked up the question, and found the right of way was real ; so he took with him some soldiers and some peasants, pulled down the gate, broke it up, and wrote on one of the bars : " Pulled up by Charles Bradlaugh, C. 52, VII D. G." The land-owner did not prosecute, and the gate did not reappear. Many another story might be told of his soldier-days, but I must hurry on to the sterner conflicts which lay before him. He left the regiment with a " very good character," respected by his officers, who had learned his value, and loved by his comrades all round.

A SIX-FOOT ERRAND BOY.

When Charles Bradlaugh once more reached London, he found his father dead, and his mother in need of help. But at first he could find no work, seek it as he might. The fine soldierly young fellow, standing six feet one and a-half inches in his stockings, with his bright and ingenuous young face and eager manners, found no place into which he could fit. At last a chance came, a chance that

few would have grasped. He sought work as a clerk from
Mr. Thomas Rogers, a solicitor in Fenchurch street, but
there was no vacancy. As he was leaving, Mr. Rogers
mentioned that he wanted an errand boy, and perhaps Mr.
Bradlaugh could recommend him one.

"What salary would you give the errand boy ?"

"Ten shillings a week."

"Then I'll take it."

"You !"

Mr. Bradlaugh has told me how astonished Mr. Rogers
was, how he suggested that the place was not suitable, and
how he himself begged to have it, humorously pleading
that his height would not prevent him from starving if he
could not get work. Mr. Rogers was at last persuaded,
and young Bradlaugh took the place. Surely the queerest
of errand boys, twenty years of age, with his great height
and soldierly bearing, with his wide reading, his knowledge
of Hebrew, Greek, Latin, Arabic and French, his now-set-
tled political and theological opinions, his mastery of
speech. But that he was willing to take the place of
errand boy at 10s. a week shows the stuff of which the
future leader was a-building, and that readiness to do any
work by which he might gain his bread honestly, never
dreaming that any form of labor could degrade him so long
as that labor was done to the best of his power. But a
young fellow of his rare ability could not long remain an
errand boy ; nine months after he entered the office he was
the head of the common law department ; and it was not
long before the tall youth, with a profound belief in his own
capacities and knowledge, was to be seen in the chambers
of judges, doing his employer's work with such marked
success, despite his boyish appearance, that the conduct of
cases rapidly fell into his hands.

Charles Bradlaugh now resumed his writing and lecturing work, and though anonymous letters denouncing his infidel clerk were showered upon Mr. Rogers, that gentleman never put on him the slightest pressure, only asking that he should not let his business suffer on account of his personal work. To meet this difficulty, Charles Bradlaugh adopted the *nom de guerre* of "Iconoclast," and under this name he wrote and spoke up to the year 1868.

A GOOD HUSBAND AND A GOOD FATHER.

In 1854 he married Miss Susannah Hooper, the daughter of one of his strongest and most devoted admirers. Mr. Hooper is still living, a very old and feeble man, but to the end "my son Charles" was his pride and glory ; he had heard the boy speak in Bonner's Fields, and watched him with unwavering admiration until the grave closed over him before his time. "He is a good man, my dear," old Mr. Hooper has often said to me ; "he was a good husband, and he is a good father. He has been too good all his life to everybody near him." No man, they say, is a hero to his *valet de chambre.* Charles Bradlaugh was a hero most of all to those who lived at his side, nearest to him in blood or friendship. It is, perhaps, the finest testimony to his worth that those who were closest to him admired him and loved him even more than any other. No man was more perfect in the home. Simple in his tastes, never grumbling about food or other trifles, content with a slice of cold meat, plenty of mustard, bread and butter, and a cup of tea—or in later years a glass of claret—there never was a complaint or a cross look. He could enjoy a good dinner if it came in his way ; he was perfectly content with the plainest of plain fare—the very easiest man to please anyone could wish for.

AUDACITY AND LEGALITY.

Now began that long series of political and theological struggles that made him so loved and trusted a leader of the democracy. As a popular leader he had two salient characteristics : consummate audacity and supreme respect for law. He would beat his foes with legal weapons, and, leading his followers into the most apparently defiant acts, he would throw over them the impenetrable shield of legal right. One of his earliest audacities showed this in marked fashion. Some poor men had saved up enough to build a little hall in Goldsmith's Row, Hackney, but they built it on freehold land without observing some formality which would have secured them in possession. The freeholder let them build, and then claimed land and building as his own. The men in their trouble went to young Charles Bradlaugh, who, finding that they were legally in the wrong, advised them to offer a rent of £25 a year. The freeholder, charmed at the prospect of obtaining a hall without build-ing it, refused to let the ground, and stood on his "rights." So Mr. Bradlaugh picked out a hundred reliable men, and pledged them to obedience and the maintenance of perfect order. He then went with them to the hall, each, carrying a shovel, a crowbar, or other convenient tool, and directed them to level the hall with the ground, and carry away ev-ery bit of the building materials. These were divided among the subscribers, and the freeholder had his land, bare as at the beginning. There was much rejoicing over the discomfiture of the enemy, but Mr. Bradlaugh advised his friends in the future to come to him before they began to build instead of when they had nearly finished.

THE PROPAGANDA OF FREETHOUGHT.

From 1854 onwards were waged the bitter conflicts by

which an organized freethought party was built up in this country. A few specimens of Mr. Bradlaugh's experiences in these years will go far to explain the occasional bitternesses of speech that, isolated from their contests, and divorced from the occasions that provoked them, were used by the baser of his opponents to exclude him from Parliament.

Wigan was one of the towns visited by Mr. Bradlaugh again and again, until he became as welcome as at first he was hated, and it may serve as an illustration of the fashion of those early combats. The local clergy stirred up in the town, before he arrived, a furious feeling against "the infidel," and the hall in which he was to lecture was crowded with a hostile audience before he reached it. The windows were broken from outside, while the crowd within yelled ; the rector's secretary forced his way in through a window, lime was thrown in, and water poured through the ventilators on the roof. Nevertheless, the lecture was delivered, but matters became more serious at the close. The crowd, composed of well-dressed people, rushed around him, from behind, spat in his face, and he was absolutely alone. But he walked through them, unyielding, defiant, and, hundreds as there were against one, his magnetic personality triumphed over their hatred. They threw stones, cursed him, yelled and hooted, but out of them all not one would meet him face to face. Time after time he went back to Wigan, until all rioting ceased and welcome grew clamorous, as courage and tenacity worked their inevitable results.

The story of Wigan is the story of a dozen other towns, in every one of which he finally won the day. Often a hearing was gained from a yelling crowd by some trick, and once gained the hearing could be kept by the orator's tongue. Thus, on one occasion, knowing he would be met by a noisy crowd, he filled his pockets with oranges. His rising to speak was the signal for an indescribable din, which no human voice could dominate, so he quietly took his oranges out of his pockets, arranged them in a row on the table, took up one and peeled and ate it. As he began upon another without any attempt at speech, curiosity began to move the crowd, and there was a moment's lull ; he lifted his eyes : " Gentlemen, will you tell me how long you are going on, so that I may know if I need send for more oranges?" It was the last thing in the world the people had expected, and they roared with laughter. In a moment he had begun his speech, captured their attention, and the lecture proceeded peaceably to its close. By courage, tact, and sheer ability, he had—when I joined the party in 1874 —so broken down violence of opposition, that I was only personally assailed with physical violence on three or four occasions, and in every large town there were some hundreds of " Bradlaugh's men," ready to keep the peace at all meetings.

THE LEGAL RIGHTS OF FREE SPEECH.

The establishment of the legal right to speak freely on religious matters was yet harder to win. Here he wore out his antagonists by legal devices, the law being against him. Thus, at Devonport he had hired a field for his lecture, all buildings in the town being refused to him, and he was arrested by Superintendent Edwards when he had only uttered the words : " Friends, I am about to address you on the Bible." He was locked up and bail refused, kept for three hours in a stone cell, without chair, light or fire, before he was allowed even into a passage where there was a stove. The charge of blasphemy broke down, the police having been in such a hurry to arrest him that they had not waited for the commission of the offense. Then a charge was trumped up of " exciting to a breach of the peace, and assaulting the constable in the execution of his duty." There were seven magistrates, all hostile ; as the witnesses for the defence were unbelievers, they were rejected one after the other as incapable of taking an oath. All looked well for the Church, when some Nonconformists, indignant at the gross and palpable injustice, came forward as witnesses, and the magistrates reluctantly refused to convict. The *Devonport Independent* speaks of the admiration excited by Mr. Bradlaugh's "remarkable precision, his calm and collected demeanor, and the ability with which he conducted his own case as well as his friend's." But still the lecture had to be delivered, and he circulated a notice that he would deliver it "near" the Devonport Park Lodge. There was an immense crowd ; the superintendent with twenty-eight policemen, the mayor with the Riot Act, soldiers in readiness to resist all attempts at rescue. Placidly came walking down to the meeting-place the young man who was the cause of all the trouble, and strolled on past it to Stonehouse Creek, where a little boat was lying. Nine feet away a larger boat was moored, and to this the equable young man was rowed. There he stood, and proceeded with the delivery of his lecture, after polite bows to the superintendent and the mayor, who knew only too well that the water in Stonehouse Creek was under the jurisdiction of Saltash, a place miles away, and that their warrants did not justify an arrest outside their jurisdiction !

BOUGHT AT A HEAVY PRICE.

The next step was an action for assault and false imprisonment against the superintendent ; it resulted in a verdict, but the special jury of Devonshire land-owners gave the atheist only a farthing damages, saddling him with heavy costs. The case was then carried to London, and pleaded in *banco*, with no further legal results save increased costs ; but it taught local authorities in future to leave freethought advocates alone, and provoked many expressions from the press in favor of free speech. The *Morning Star* called it "a flagrant denial and mockery of justice," and even *Punch* protested against "magistrates becoming judges of controversy and the policemen enforcing their decrees." The suit was one of the many in which he gained much for Liberty but nothing for himself, save a load of debt which kept him always a poor man ; and though friends all over the country again and again raised money to reimburse the expenditure thus incurred, the debts were only lightened, not wiped out, and one of the heaviest losses caused by such fights in late years—the canceling of lecturing engagements and paralyzing of work necessary for the earning of his living—was never taken into account at all.

So much has been said of the supposed change in his methods of advocacy in his later years, that it seems as well to quote here, where it will reach so many who knew him not, the following from his own pen in his journal, the *National Reformer*, in February, 1863. Surely, this is not the writing of an uncultured man, brutal and coarse in his controversial methods :

"I am an infidel, a rough, self-taught infidel. What honors shall I win if I grow gray in this career ? Critics who break a lance against me in my absence, will tell you now that I am from the lower classes, without university education, and that I lack classical lore. Clergymen, who see God's mercy reflected in an eternal hell, will tell you even that I am wanting in a conception of common humanity. Skilled penmen will demonstrate that I have not the merest rudiments of biblical knowledge. I thank these assailants for the past ; when they pricked and stung me with their very waspish piety, they did me good service,

gave me the clue to my weaknesses, laid bare to me my
ignorance, and drove me to acquire knowledge which might
otherwise never have been mine. I pray the opposing
forces to continue their attacks, that by teaching me my
weakness they may make me strong. Some (who have no
taste for the excavating, tunneling and leveling work, but
are vain of having shaken hands, or takeu wine, with the
chairman of a completed line of railway) say : 'Oh ! a
mere puller-down !' Is this so ? I have preached ' equality,' not by aiming to reduce men's intellects to the level of
my own, but rather by inciting each of my hearers to
develop his mind to the fullest extent, obtaining thus the
hope, not of an equality of ignorance, but of a more equal
diffusion of knowledge. I have attacked the Bible, but
never the letter alone ; the Church, but never have I con-
fined myself to a mere assault on its practices. I have
deemed that I attacked theology best in asserting most of
the fullness of humanity. I have regarded iconoclasticism
as a means, not as an end. The work is weary, but the end
is well. The political prisoner in the Austrian dungeon
day by day filed at the massive chain and sturdy bar. The
labor is serious, but the reward is great. Tell him it is
poor drudgery work, and he tells you, ' But I toil for freedom !' Watch another captive, how, with an old nail,
rusted and rotten, he picks, atom by atom, the mortar from
between the stones of his prison wall. Tell him that other
men have used more perfect tools ; he will answer, ' This
old red-rusty nail is to me bright silver lever, powerful in-
strument, for it is the only tool I have wherewith to toil for
liberty.' Tell the backwoodsman who, with axe in hand,
hews at the trunks of sturdy trees, that his is destructive
work, and he will answer, ' I clear the ground that plough
and reaping-hook may be used by and by.' And I answer
that in many men—and women too, alas !—thought is prison-

bound with massive chains of old-church welding ; that human capacity for progress, is hindered, grated in by prison-bars, priest-wrought and law-protected ; that the good wide field of common humanity is over-crowded with the trunks of vast creed frauds, the outgrowth of ancient mythologies. I affirm that file, old nail, and axe are useful, and their use honorable, not as an end, but as some means toward the end for which all true men should strive—that is, the enduring happiness of mankind."

UNCHRISTLIKE CHRISTIANS.

So wrote Charles Bradlaugh, surely not unworthily, just eight-and-twenty years ago. Was this the language of an ignoramus, an untrained thinker, a brutal controversialist ? It may be asked, "But why, if he were such as you depict, should he have aroused such bitter hatred, and have earned such a reputation?" The answer is not far to seek. When he began his iconoclastic work, orthodoxy was rigid and imperious, and any who challenged the inspiration of the Bible, eternal torture, or vicarious atonement, were looked on as men of foul lives, seeking cover for sin in license of criticism. No one waited to hear before condemning, to examine before denouncing. He was " an infidel." It was enough. Clergy incited their flocks to mob him, to break the windows of the hall he lectured in, of the house that sheltered him, and if amid a crowd of howling believers, yelled at, cursed, struck, he let fall some biting sarcasm, some bitter jibe, it was caught up, repeated, exaggerated, and scattered broadcast as representing his general style of advocacy, without a syllable of the circumstances in the midst of which it was flung forth.

To-day, largely because of ·the work this man has done for liberty, thought and criticism have become so free that they seem a matter of course, and younger men cannot understand that the Charles Bradlaugh they knew was the Charles Bradlaugh of thirty odd years ago ; they think he has changed, when it is he who has changed public opinion. If Dr. Momerie could preach from the chapel of the Foundling Hospital doctrines that fifty years ago would have landed him in jail, he has to thank for his liberty Charles Bradlaugh and that band of men whom he inspired and led.

The tone of the opposition encountered by him may be judged by the following letter, which he printed in the *National Reformer :* •

NEWCHURCH, May 1, 1865.

DEAR SIR :
I was in company with Mr. Verity yesterday, and laid the contents of your letter before him, and although I deem it low and contemptible to take any notice of individuals who are ever and anon crying out against Christianity, yet for the sake of indulging you in your worse than beast-like propensities, I am instructed to inform you that Mr. Verity is waiting to hear from Mr. Bradlaugh, or any other fool who happens to be so mad as to imbibe your empty notions. Yours,
THOS. FIELDEN.

The "fool's" answer was, at least, more gracefully worded :—

Mr. Verity must be a pleasant man to encounter if he instructed Mr. Fielden to write the above, and, in any case, the prospect of meeting a teacher whose disciple pens such an epistle is an enticing one. My message to him is to accustom himself to a more gentlemanly and less scriptural style of communication. Coarseness is not necessarily a virtue ; in a costermonger or a piously miseducated parson it is to be looked for ; in a public speaker or writer it is better avoided.

IN HYDE PARK AND TRAFALGAR SQUARE.

His political work was as energetic during all these years, if not more energetic, than his anti-theological propaganda. He came prominently before the country in 1855, when he gave evidence before the Royal Commission appointed to inquire into the disturbances at Hyde Park in that year ; his quiet statement that he went to the park because Sir Richard Mayne had prohibited the meeting—" I had not heard then, and have not heard now, that Sir Richard Mayne has any power to forbid my going into the park, *therefore I went* "—his urbane offer to show the Commissioner how to unhorse an aggressive policeman, if one who was present would mount his horse then standing below in Palace Yard, attracted much attention at the time.

In the Reform agitation he played a prominent part, and many a tale is told by London reformers of those exciting days ; how he charged on horseback up the steps of Trafalgar Square to stop some stone-throwing that had been begun near the National Gallery, and that might have grown in a few minutes into a riot impossible to quell ; how he frustrated attempts to break their processions, on one occasion having a hansom cab, with a protesting "swell" inside, lifted off its wheels, carried bodily away, and deposited in a side street ; how he cleared out a corner where a number of thieves had congregated, with a heavy riding whip as his weapon ; how he stopped the commencing fight when the Hyde Park railings went down. All these stories and many more are written in the loving memories of those who followed him and found him always brave and true. And they delight to tell how he would defy unfair authority under shield of law.

READY TO REPEL FORCE WITH FORCE.

Thus a great meeting was called in Trafalgar Square, while Parliament was sitting, to protest against action taken in the House of Commons—a quite illegal thing. The meeting was forbidden, the promoters in despair. They went to Charles Bradlaugh ; he called the meeting, merely changing the form in which the object was couched, making it legal instead of illegal, and defied the authorities to break it up. So again, with a forbidden Hyde Park meeting, he informed the police of his intention ; sent for by a statesman high in office, he repeated his determination ; told that the meeting would be broken up by the soldiers, he gravely thanked his informant for the warning, saying that he would not lead unarmed men into danger of being shot down ; that he would not be the first to use violence, but that if violence were illegally committed on the people, peacefully assembled in legal meeting, he would repel force by force. Said with his peculiar slow gravity, with level-fronting eyes, the menace would not fail of its full weight: The statesman understood, the meeting was held, and no attack was made. But he had taken all his precautions. Two hundred men were around him, ready to obey him, and had the soldiers been wickedly sent out to fire on the people, he was ready, as he said, to repel force by force, to guard the people who trusted him and answered to his summons.

HIS SYMPATHIES WITH FRANCE.

In foreign politics he took an active part, aiding in the famous defense of Dr. Simon Bernard in 1859, and in the same year delivering a lecture against the French Emperor that so disturbed the occupant of the Tuilleries that representations were made to the English Government, and the

London hall engaged for the lecture was taken possession of by the police. He hated Louis Napoleon as he hated few men : "*Le sang de mes amis*," he wrote, "*etait sur son âme.*"

But when Napoleon fell, he threw himself, heart and soul, into an agitation to prevent the English alliance with Germany for which the English Court was believed to be working, and that so successfully that he was publicly thanked by the Government of National Defense, which wrote him that in France he would always be *concitoyen*. For Prince Napoleon (Jerome) he had a real affection, regarding him as exceptionally able and as a man of the greatest possibilities ; but he would often be angered by the indolence with which his own active nature had no sympathy, and by the folly which would let some trivial amusement draw him away from great affairs of State.

AN ITALIAN ADVENTURE.

Italy, too, he served in the days ere Italy became again a nation. For Mazzini he entertained a positive veneration. "I would have died for that man," he has said to me—only wishing that some worldly insight into men's characters could have been added to the courage of the hero and the loftiness of the saint. Carrying letters from Italy to Mazzini in which men's lives were hidden, he once nearly lost his own. The Papal gendarmes boarded the vessel in which he was, and, all persuasion failing, he was at last compelled to draw his revolver ; none dared attack him in front, but they would have captured him from behind had not a plucky American sprung to his help and placed his back against Charles Bradlaugh's, arming himself with a chair as a weapon. The gendarmes departed for further orders, and the ship was out of reach ere they could return.

He had one purely comical adventure, interesting only in

showing the readiness with which he could extricate himself from a difficulty. The police at Montalbo tried to deprive him of his revolver, on the ground that the carrying of revolvers was forbidden by the Italian law. Having already found it useful, he declined to give it up, and a struggle for its possession was imminent, owner and policeman both hanging on to it ; in a moment he was seized from all sides, and was obliged to fall back on argument, so he carefully explained that he had insured his life in the Life Assurance Company, and had to do with the Sovereign and Midland Assurance Company as well, so that he was bound to defend his life and carry arms. This argument was too much for the police, who carefully took down the imposing titles and promptly released him, revolver and all !

A KNIGHT-ERRANT OF LIBERTY IN SPAIN.

When Spain made her short-lived republic, this knight-errant of liberty went to Madrid, in 1873, crossing the Carlist lines at peril of life, meeting with some curious and dangerous adventures—as when he requisitioned an old chaise, and telling the driver that if he stopped on *any* pretext he would shoot him, and the driver went on at a furious gallop despite yells and stray musket-balls from Carlist scouts, rightly judging that the bullet in the revolver behind him in the grip of the stern-speaking Englishman was more dangerous than the ill-aimed shots of his countrymen—but reaching Madrid safely and delivering to Castelar a letter with which he was charged from the great Republican meeting at Birmingham. "Caballero Bradlaugh" was heartily welcomed at Madrid, and a state banquet was given in his honor, and he made at it a remarkable speech, of which the last sentences may be given here. He had expressed the hope that at the end of twenty years England might be republican, and he concluded :

"Speaking for myself, I may answer that if a republic could come to-morrow in England, without force, without blood-shed, without crime, without ruined cities and anger-maddened peoples, then I would be the first to greet it and to serve it ; but our republic will, I trust, come nursed by the school, the brain, the pen, and the tongue, and not heralded by the cannon's roar or carved by the sword. Hence it is that I say I should prefer to work, even for twenty years, to strengthen men's brains, so that they may know how to keep the republic when they have won it, and that it may be an indestructible republic, which shall honor the destinies of the people of England, and serve as guide as well as mother to the English-speaking races throughout the world."

I am told that Castelar, baited by a group of Intransigeantes, at last angrily told them that Bradlaugh, the red-hot English Republican, was far more reasonable than they, and that if they had understood the speech he made they would have thrown him out of the window instead of cheering him !

HIS WORK FOR IRELAND.

While thus aiding foreign people in their struggles toward liberty, he did not forget a people nearer home. He recognized in Ireland the same rights that he pleaded for in France, in Spain, in Italy ; he took part in the agitation that culminated in the Fenian movement, and drafted the famous manifesto—except the proclamation of an Irish republic, which he protested against as impracticable, and therefore idle—of "The Irish People to the World." He has told me much of the secret history of this movement, of its leaders, the faithful and the betrayers ; but as there are still some people living who might suffer from the recital, however interesting and valuable from a historical stand-point, I have, as yet, no right to break silence.

It must suffice to say that he regarded the suspension of the Habeas Corpus Act as justifying forcible resistance to the Executive, which thus became tyrant instead of constitutional ruler ; and though Corydon's personal fear of the consequences prevented him from betraying Mr. Bradlaugh as he betrayed others, Mr. Bradlaugh's connection with the movement was so well known to the authorities that he was closely watched by the police, who, however, found themselves foiled by their acute quarry. In 1878, we find him earnestly urging union between the Irish party and the English Radical party, pleading then, as he had pleaded for three and twenty years, for justice to and freedom for Ireland.

THE FREETHINKER'S CLAIM TO AFFIRM.

His legal conflicts, maintained through all these years of public activity, were many and great. Apart from all the minor struggles, like those at Devonport, he had two great and prolonged battles, one on oaths in courts of justice, the other on freedom of the newspaper press.

He was concerned first with one or two cases in which other freethinkers and he himself suffered injustice because the law permitted them neither to swear nor to affirm. In 1867 a Christian named DeRin, who was largely in debt to Mr. Bradlaugh, sought to escape the payment of the debt under cover of the legal incapacity of his creditor to swear in its proof. The battle was waged in many courts. In one the judges refused to hear Mr. Bradlaugh except upon affidavit, and he was incompetent to make an affidavit ; in another, he could not give evidence ; the case dragged on wearily, the indefatigable atheist finding new ground on which to proceed after every defeat.

Meanwhile, he petitioned Parliament, he agitated through the press, and in 1870 then won his case, but the defendant promptly became bankrupt, so Mr. Bradlaugh never got his debt, and was left crippled with the enormous costs of the three years' struggle. The freethinker became a competent witness, but the champion was left crushed by a load of debt. So in the later oath struggle, the way to all future freethinkers is open, but he has paid toll with his life.

HIS SERVICES TO LIBERTY OF THE PRESS.

The other great conflict was against giving £400 surety against the appearance of blasphemous or seditious articles in a newspaper published at less than sixpence. The law was one of the Georgian statutes, designed to prevent a free press. Mr. Bradlaugh had refused to give these sureties on the ground that he would forfeit them in every issue of his paper, and he was not rich enough to conduct the paper at so heavy a cost. He was prosecuted, and penalties of £20 per copy issued were claimed. He politely answered that he did not keep so much money at his bank—the paper had been issued weekly for eight years—and printed on his paper, "Prosecuted by Her Majesty's Attorney-General." The battle was long, and he tripped up the Crown over and over again—the whole story ought to be read in detail by those who would understand his extraordinary readiness and address—till at last the prosecution broke down.

Just then the Tory Government went out of office, and the Liberals came in. The prosecution was again commenced, and again fought by the undaunted editor, until a bill was brought in repealing the statute under which he was prosecuted, and a *stet processus* was entered by the Crown. John Stuart Mill wrote to the victorious combatant a warm letter of congratulation, saying that "You have gained a very honorable success in obtaining a repeal of the mischievous Act by your persevering resistance."

DEBTS AND DIFFICULTIES.

Victorious, yes ; but again, at what a cost ! The last stroke of financial ruin came to him in his business, large orders given were thrown back on his hands when the customers found he was " Bradlaugh the Atheist," and he consequently determined to give up all business and trust to his tongue and pen for his livelihood. His liabilities were enormous, but his honor was so trusted that he was able to avoid bankruptcy by his personal promise to pay if time were given him. He sold everything he possessed except his books ; his home that he had got together by hard work, his furniture, even a diamond ring given him by a grateful person whom he had helped. He sent his children to school ; his wife, not physically able to bear the life he faced, went to live with her parents in the country, and he took two small rooms in Turner Street, Whitechapel, for which he paid 3s. 6d. a week, and where he remained until he had cleared off most of his liabilities. He then moved to lodgings over a music shop in Circus Road, St. John's Wood, where he lived for the remainder of his life, his daughters joining him on the death of their mother in 1877. When he died he left behind him not one personal debt ; all who had trusted to honor found their claims discharged. He died poor indeed, with no personal property save his library, his Indian gifts, and his very modest wardrobe : but he left his name free, his honor unstained.

MR. BRADLAUGH IN AMERICA.

Part of his debts he cleared off by lectures delivered in America. There he was an immense favorite, both as speaker and as man. From the New York customs officer over his luggage, as he chalked it without examination, "Mr. Bradlaugh, we know you here, and the least we can do for you is to pass you through comfortably," to the greatest literary men of the States, all united to do him honor. The Lotos Club welcomed him as a most honored guest, and he met there a crowd of celebrities. At Boston, Wendell Phillips took the chair at his first lecture, Charles Sumner gave him public greeting, and William Lloyd Garrison marked his approbation. He met Ralph Waldo Emerson, his boyish idol, at a reception given in his honor; made friends with Bret Harte, Washburne, Vice-President Wilson, Joshua B. Smith (the colored senator), and many another good and great man.

Twice again he visited America, on the last occasion nearly leaving his life there. He had a terrible attack of pleurisy and typhoid, but was tended with rare skill by Drs. Otis, Leaming and Abbe, at St. Luke's Hospital, New York. His life was despaired of, and he lay facing death with the absolute serenity characteristic of him. His patient fortitude and perfect calmness saved him, they said. He told me that he had one terrible struggle at the idea of giving up life and work, and the friends he dearly loved; but he fought it down and conquered—tender as his heart was, his great fortitude could master it—and not one thought of regret touched him again. Open-eyed, he faced death and measured the grave in his pathway; desiring to live, but not afraid to die, he lay patient, brave, hopeful always. As to his opinions, the very possibility of changing them never came within the range of his thought, either then or at any other time. Thrice, ere the final blow fell, he looked into the eyes of Death and blanched not. Opinions that were good enough to guide through life's complex problems were, to his brave, straightforward nature, quite good enough for facing the simple stroke of death.

MR. BRADLAUGH AS A FRIEND.

My personal acquaintance with Mr. Bradlaugh dates from 1874 ; and I take leave to say that while others have known him longer, none have known him so intimately as I —in his hopes and his fears, his motives and his dreams, his past, which he unrolled to me in every public and private detail as a book, his future plans, which now may never be worked to their foreseen ends.

Some fancy that he was always grave. Before 1881 he was the veriest boy in his hours of relaxation, full of merry jokes and gaiety, overbrimming with fun. How many bright memories I have of our excursions together, a few hours snatched from our busy lives, in which all business was forgotten and time ran on golden wheels ! Most often fishing was the amusement—his one passion in the way of relaxation—and he taught me the mysteries of the craft, but always considered it a deficiency in my character that I never cared to fish by myself. Often the fishing rod would be left behind, and we would walk or drive, wandering far through Richmond Park, sitting under the splendid trees, and discussing the days of the then future, when he should be lawmaker and play his part in the council of the nation. We never doubted that those days would come ; we always realized that the opposition would be bitter, and the victory delayed ; but in all our outlooks over the future we never saw August 3, 1881, nor caught glimpse of the injustice that brought him, prematurely aged, to his grave. How he would often voice his love of England, his admiration of her Parliament, his pride in her history. Keenly alive to the blots upon it in her sinful wars of conquest, and cruel wrongs inflicted upon subject peoples, he was yet an Englishman to the heart's core, but feeling, above all, the Englishman's duty, as one of a race that had gripped power and held it, to understand the needs of those he ruled, and do justice, since compulsion to justice there was none. His service to India of late years was no suddenly accepted task. He had spoken for her, pleaded for her, for many a long year, through press and on platform, and his spurs as member for India were won long ere he was Member of Parliament.

HIS COURTESY TO WOMEN.

One trait of his character was very noticeable and very attractive—his extreme courtesy, especially to women. This outward polish, which sat so gracefully on his massive frame and stately presence, was foreign rather than English —the English being, as a rule, save among those who go to Court, a singularly unpolished people—and gave his manner a peculiar charm. I asked him once where he had learned his gracious fashions that were so un-English, and he answered, with a half smile, half scoff, that it was only in England that he was an outcast from society. In France, in Spain, in Italy, he was always welcomed among men and women of the highest social rank, and he supposed that he had unconsciously caught the foreign tricks of manner. Moreover, he was absolutely indifferent to all questions of social position ; peer or artisan, it was to him exactly the same ; he never seemed conscious of the distinctions of which men make so much.

How much I personally owe him for wise criticism, helpful guidance, careful judgment, it is quite impossible for me to say. He used to be my sternest, as well as gentlest critic, telling me that in a party like ours, where our own education and knowledge were above those whom we led, it was very easy to gain indiscriminate praise and unbounded admiration ; on the other hand, from Christians we received equally indiscriminate abuse and hatred. It was needful then to be our own harshest judges, and to be sure we knew thoroughly every subject that we taught. At the time when I discovered that I had the gift of speech, and began to taste the intoxication of easy won applause, his criticism and trained judgment were of priceless service to me, and what of value there is in my work is very largely due to his influence, which at once stimulated and restrained.

THE STORY OF A FAMOUS TRIAL.

In 1877 came the famous " Knowlton trial," a trial that cost him more of pain and loss than any other act in his life, and brought out his noblest qualities. The story is simple enough. Dr. Charles Knowlton was an American physician, of respectable standing, convinced of the truth of the teaching of the Rev. Mr. Malthus, and seeing that it was practically futile unless married people were taught to limit their families within their means of livelihood, he wrote, early in the present century (some time in the thirties), a book on the limitation of the family, entitled the "Fruits of Philosophy." The book circulated in America and in England, but not very largely. At the close of 1876, it was suddenly attached at Bristol, and at the beginning of 1877 its London publisher, Mr. Charles Watts, who published also for Mr. Bradlaugh and myself, was prosecuted for it as an obscene book. He pleaded guilty, to our great wrath and dismay ; and as the question was of immense public importance, being nothing less than the right of giving to the poor important information at a low price, we determined to become publishers and re-issue the pamphlet. We recognized the horrible misconceptions that would probably arise ; he believed that he was forfeiting all hope of sitting for Northampton ; but the cry of the poor was in our ears, aud we could not permit the discussion of the population question, in its one practical aspect, to be crushed.

We did not like the pamphlet, but to stop it was to stop all. We took a shop, printed the tract, sent notice to the police that we would personally sell it to them, and did so. We were arrested and committed for trial. We moved the action to the Court of Queen's Bench by writ of *certiorari*, granted after Lord Chief Justice Cockburn had read the pamphlet, saying that if it were an obscene book in the ordinary sense of the word he would refuse the writ. We were tried ; the Lord Chief Justice summed up strongly, very strongly, for an acquittal, but the jury brought in a verdict condemning the book, while "completely exonerating" us from any wrong intent. This the judge reluctantly translated into a verdict of guilty, and then let us go on our own recognizances for a week. Subsequently, the judge said he would have let us go if we would have submitted to the Court, but as we insisted on being contumacious, he must sentence us to a fine and imprisonment. After which he set us free, on our own recognizances again, to appeal on a point of law, we promising not to sell pending the appeal. The appeal was successful, the sentence quashed, and we recommenced the sale.

Then Mr. Bradlaugh took the aggressive, and commenced an action against the police for retaining our property, the pamphlets seized. He was successful, recovered the pamphlets, and sold them marked "Recovered from the police." The sale continued for some time. At last we received an intimation that no further prosecution would be attempted, and we then at once dropped the sale of the book. I wrote a pamphlet containing all the information given by Dr. Knowlton, but less antiquated and more concise ; it has had an immense circulation, and no prosecution against it has ever been attempted here. In New South Wales it was attacked, but was vindicated in a most luminous judgment by Justice Windmeyer, of the Supreme Court — a judgment that we reprinted here, as our complete justification. So ended a terrible struggle, in which indeed we suffered bitterly and were fouled by every insult that profligates could formulate, but in which we gave the poor knowledge that has raised thousands out of direst poverty, and saved thousands of poor men's wives from despair.

A NOBLE LIFE.

With this hardly-won victory, I close these poor notes on a noble life. From 1880 onwards all the world knows how Charles Bradlaugh fought, how he won his right, how he passed his Oaths Act, how he made his mark in Parliament, how the world caught some glimpse of the real man, how the Commons made him amends as he lay dying, how one cry of regret went up beside his grave, how England's greatest Minister spoke of him, erstwhile despised and hated, as "that distinguished man and useful member of this House." Man of unswerving principle and unflinching courage, of noble ambition and unfaltering will, of keen insight and strong grasp, of laborious patience and overmastering eloquence, he would have done yeoman service to his country had he lived, but he would have been no greater man, nor left an example more inspiring. To us who loved him the loss is irremediable, and England will seek long ere she find a sturdier and more loyal son. Without faith in God, but full of love to man, he led a pure and noble life, and he has won the only immortality his strong soul craved, the memory of honest service, faithfully wrought, loyally rendered—deathless memory in a world made nobler by his living, richer by his sacrifices, poorer by his death.